# Mama Kangaroo

## NURSERY RHYMES
## FOR
## MODERN TIMES

**By Cassandra Lennox**

**Illustrated by Jasmine Mills**

Mama Kangaroo Nursery Rhymes for Modern Times by Cassandra Lennox

For information regarding permission, write to:

Cassandra Lennox
P.O. Box 1447
Wilkes-Barre, Pa 18703

First Printing: March 2018
Printed in the United States of America

Write World Press

ISBN 978-1-7328017-0-7

www.mamakangaroo.site
facebook.com/mamakangaroobooks
cassandra@mamakangaroo.site

For Mama's Little Kangaroos-

Joey, Lily, Cayley & Tyler

THANK YOU-

*To my wonderful children
for being the inspiration for Mama Kangaroo.*

*To my husband Joe and my family
for their continued encouragement and support.*

*To my tribe of moms and their beautiful babies.*

&

*To Jasmine, for her incredible talent
and help in achieving this dream.*

I'll tell you a story,
Sing you a song,
Read you a rhyme,
And you'll join along.

Let you find comfort,
Help you to learn,
Laugh along with you
With each page we turn.

Times have changed,
And rhymes can, too.
To all today's children,
These are for you!

Dream big, sweet child.
You can touch the sky.
It all begins with a lullaby.
Then you learn and then you grow,
There's so much you'll come to know.

Dream great, sweet child.
You can go so far.
It begins when you reach for a star.
Then you grasp your dream within your hand,
There's so much you'll come to understand.

Dream grand, sweet child.
I believe in you.
It begins when your wishes come true.
Then there's a whole world to see,
There's so much you'll someday be…

Rub a dub dub, 3 ducks in the tub,
What color do you think they'd be?
Yellow and blue and a pink one, too.
"Quack, quack, quack," say all three.

Ring around the rosies, spin from head to toesies.
Dizzy, dizzy, we all fall down!

Little Elephant Ellie
Had a rumbly belly,
And was eating her PB&J.
Along came a mouse,
Right into her house,
And frightened poor Ellie away!

Star light, star bright,
Prettiest star in the sky tonight.
Sparkling silver in a sky of blue,
Please grant my wish come true.

The itsy bitsy turtles were eggs under the sand.
"Crack" went the shells and they crawled onto the land.
Up came the tide to set the babies free,
And the itsy bitsy turtles ventured out to sea.

Sugar cookies warm,

Sugar cookies cold.

Sugar cookies gobbled up won't get old.

Some like them warm,

Some like them cold.

All like to eat them up before they're old.

Silly Billy
Climbed up a wall.
Silly Billy had a big fall!
All of his family and all of his friends,
Told Billy not to climb the walls again!

Hey Diddle, Diddle,
The monkey in the middle,
The ball flew over his head.
So swung from a tree
And grabbed it did he,
Then his friend was a monkey instead!

Rock a bye baby, in Mommy's embrace,
In cute little jammies and a smile on your face.
When the day's over and stars start to glow,
Sweet little baby to dreamland will go.

Hickory, Dickory, Delight,
The sun comes up so bright,
The day goes on,
And then is gone,
The moon says now it is night.

Eenie,
meeny,
miney,
moe.
Which to choose I do not know.
I'll let this decide it so,
Eenie, meeny, miney, moe.

What are little ones made of?
Sweetest of dreams
and bright moon beams.
Hugs and kisses
and birthday wishes.
The sun from above
and bundles of love.
That's what little ones are made of!

Hush little baby, don't you cry.

Daddy's gonna sing you a lullaby.

And if that lullaby is not enough,

Daddy's gonna make your face light up.

And if there's still not a smile on your face,

Daddy's gonna give you a sweet embrace.

And if that hug doesn't do the trick,

Daddy's gonna warm some milk real quick.

And if that milk won't help you nap,

Daddy's gonna rock you on his lap.

And if after all that you still cry,

Daddy's gonna call for Mommy to try!

One, Two - It's a day anew.

Three, Four - Time to play once more.

Five, Six - Now a meal to fix.

Seven, Eight - It's getting late.

Nine, Ten - Time to sleep again.

The girls and boys have lost their toys
And don't know where to find them.
If they put them away, there they'll stay,
And Mom won't need to remind them!

Dance, little baby, no need to fear.

Don't worry baby, Mama's here.

A giggle and laugh and smile so bright,

There, little baby, such delight!

Way up high and way down low,

I'll hold you tight and around we go.

Dance little baby and together we'll sing,

And we'll find joy in everything!

Girls and boys go out and play,

Be it evening or be it day.

Leave your games and tv without a care,

And join your friends for nice fresh air.

Come with laughter and with a smile.

Take your time and stay a while.

In the yard or in the park,

Until the streetlights signal dark.

Ride on a bike to a house up the block,
To see a good friend and have a nice talk.
Rings on her fingers and hair up in bows,
She will make friends wherever she goes.

Mandy, Mandy, oh so handy,
How does your garden grow?
Sweet peas, pink lilies,
And daffodils all in a row.

Look around, what colors do you see?
Green like the leaves up on a tree?
Red like apples, or a ripe strawberry,
Blue blueberries, or a yellow canary?

Look all around, what shapes do you see?
Round like the sun, a ball or a pea?
Square or rectangle like a cardboard box,
Or triangles like the ears of a fox?

It's raining, it's snowing.
It's chilly and blowing.
Jump in bed,
Where it's warm instead.
And stay cuddled up till the morning.

When you use your imagination,
Every day is a new creation.

Playing house,
A castle of blocks.
Tents made of blankets,
An animal that talks.

Stories in books,
Families of dolls.
Puzzles and cars
Or bats and balls.

Creating a world
With markers and crayons,
Dress up like characters
From faraway lands.

The possibilities have no end,
When you imagine and play pretend!

Mama Kangaroo and her sweet little crew
Got all tucked in and ready for night.
She read them some rhymes,
And kissed each 3 times,
To last them till morning light.

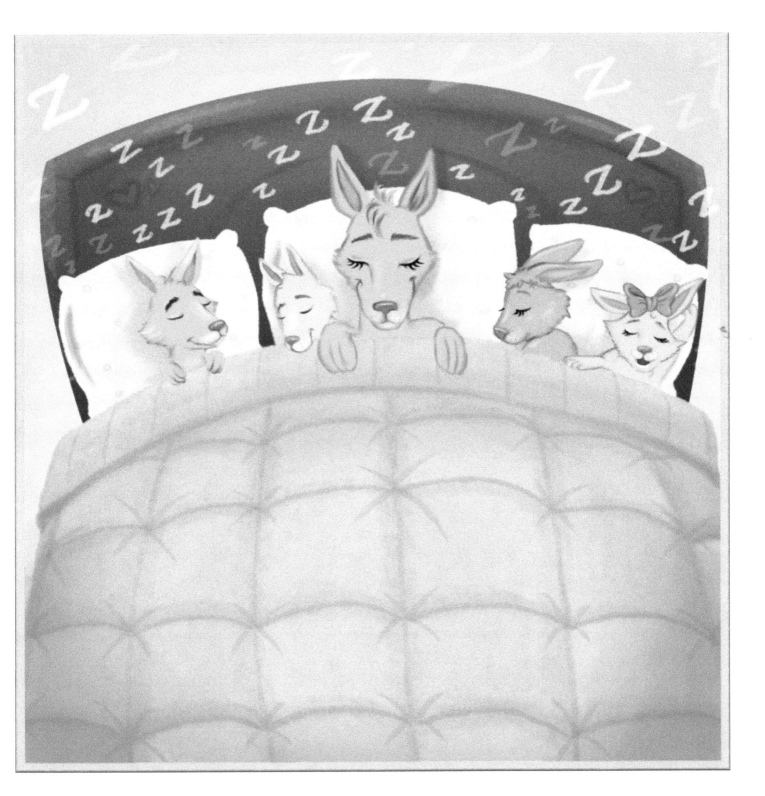

## About the Author

*Pennsylvania author Cassandra Lennox began writing at the age of 8. In addition to creating books for children, she also writes novels, poetry, quotes, and journals for adults and teenagers. Her mission with her writing is to inspire, educate, and entertain while provoking thought and conveying emotion. She loves to make others smile and motivate them to chase their dreams. Cassandra enjoys spending time with her children and husband, reading, gardening, cooking, traveling, playing board games, and embracing every moment on these beautifully crazy journeys of writing and motherhood!*

## About the Illustrator

*Virginia artist Jasmine Mills crafts distinctly American pieces. They explore the varied textures of life in a land between north and south, mountains and sea, past and progress. They merge genre, mixed media, and redraw stylistic boundaries. Jasmine works in traditional media, digital art and illustration and art licensing. She is an art teacher at the Petersburg Area Art League and summer camp instructor. A portion of her gallery show proceeds are donated to the Children's Hospital of Richmond.*

CPSIA information can be obtained
at www.ICGtesting.com
Printed in the USA
BVHW011330110319
542311BV00004B/66/P

9 781732 801721